Arthur and the Seventh-Inning Stretcher

A Marc Brown **GOOD SPORTS** Chapter Book

Arthur and the Seventh-Inning Stretcher

Text by Stephen Krensky

1837

Little, Brown and Company

Boston   New York   London

Chapter 1

• • • • • • • • • • •

"You're late," said Arthur.

He was talking to Buster, who had just arrived for the first baseball practice of the season.

Buster yawned. "I'm not used to getting up so early on Saturdays."

"Neither am I," Arthur admitted. "But D.W. woke me at the crack of dawn. She's very excited about being the Eagles' team batgirl. I tried to explain to her that we didn't have to be the first ones here, but she wouldn't listen. 'Batgirls have to set a good example,' she said."

"A good example for what?" asked Francine, riding up on her bike.

Arthur explained about D.W.

"Well, I always set a good example on the baseball diamond," said Francine. "Great pitching. Timely hitting. And I look quite nice on a baseball card, too. Number seven, that's me."

"You've already picked out your number?" asked the Brain.

"Of course. I don't like it too high or too low. And double digits are bad."

"Why?"

"The extra number weighs you down. Pitchers need to stay light on their feet."

"Actually," said the Brain, "I don't believe that the additional weight on the back of your shirt influences —"

"Attention, everyone!" shouted Coach Frensky, Francine's dad. He welcomed them to the first practice and outlined his hopes for the season. "Play hard, have fun, and be careful," he told them. "Remember those three things and we'll all have a great time."

He then divided the team into pairs and instructed them to warm up. Everyone had a partner except the Brain.

"You'll be with Binky," said the coach, "as soon as he gets here."

Binky arrived a few minutes later. "Coach says we're paired up," he said, looking down at the Brain, who was sitting on the grass.

The Brain nodded. "You're late."

Binky shrugged. "I didn't miss anything important." He punched his glove. "Come on, Brain. Let's get started."

"I *have* started," the Brain said. "I'm stretching."

"Oh, come on, that stuff is boring. How long will it take?" said Binky.

"Just a few minutes," said the Brain.

Binky scratched his head. "Yeah, yeah. Are you done yet?"

"Patience, Binky. Some things can't be rushed."

"But I've been ready for hours," Binky complained.

"It hasn't been hours, Binky. You just got here."

"Well, it seems like hours. Maybe they were just really long minutes. I want to get moving." Binky closed his eyes.

"Who's that coming up to the plate?"

"I can't tell. He's moving so fast, he's just a blur. Oh, wait, he's stopped now. It's Binky Barnes, the fastest boy alive."

"I hear he won six races at the state track meet last week."

"That's right. Look how he stands at the plate. What a stance! Such concentration."

Craaack!

"It's a slow dribbler to the shortstop, but

look at Binky go! He's already passed second. The shortstop has the ball now. . . . Binky's rounding third. The throw to the plate. . . . Not in time! Binky Barnes has just hit the first infield home run."

"Okay, Binky, I'm ready," said the Brain.

Binky grunted. "It's about time."

Chapter 2

• • • • • • • • • • • •

At dinner that evening, Arthur slowly lowered himself into his chair.

"Feeling the effects of the first practice, eh?" said his father, putting the casserole on the table.

Arthur groaned. "All of my muscles forgot everything they learned last year. My whole body feels like spaghetti." He gripped the table. "If I don't hold on tight, I'll probably slide right onto the floor."

His mother smiled. "Don't worry. Your muscles will come around soon enough."

"My muscles feel fine," said D.W. "I was

born to be a batgirl. I worked my way up to two bats on each shoulder."

Mrs. Read frowned. "You be careful, D.W. Bats are heavier than they look."

"How's your team doing?" asked Mr. Read.

"Pretty well," said Arthur. "We —"

"Let me tell, Arthur!" said D.W. "Francine's trying to develop a breaking ball. Muffy won't slide because she doesn't like to get her uniform dirty. Buster gets dizzy in the outfield." She paused for breath. "And you should see Binky run. He's as fast as lightning or thunder or —"

"Thunder isn't fast, D.W.," said Arthur. "That's why we see the lightning first."

"Okay, lightning, then. He gets this fierce look on his face where he's biting down on his lip — and then he just takes off! He doesn't even have to warm up or anything."

"But that isn't good," said Arthur.

"You're just jealous," said D.W. "You wish you could run that fast."

"Hold on there, D.W.," said Mr. Read. "Arthur doesn't have to be jealous to be concerned about Binky. When I was your age, there was a kid in our neighborhood called Flex Logan. His real name was Chester, but no one ever called him that. The reason we called him Flex was that he could bend his arms and legs all around like a pretzel."

"Why didn't you call him Pretzel?" asked D.W.

"I don't know. We just didn't. Anyway, Flex always used to make sure his arms and legs were good and loose before he tried any tricks. But one day he was in a hurry. He was doing this thing where he bent both his feet up behind his neck."

"Did he make it?" Arthur asked.

"Oh, he made it all right. But then he got cramps in both legs and couldn't untie himself. An ambulance had to come and take him to the hospital."

"Was he okay?" asked Arthur.

"Eventually. They had to put him in a huge whirlpool of warm water until his muscles finally relaxed."

"So he completely recovered?" said Arthur.

Mr. Read paused. "Well, yes and no. Certainly, his body was as stretchy as ever. But . . ."

"But?" said Arthur.

"He never ate another pretzel again."

Arthur and D.W. looked at each other and groaned.

Chapter 3

• • • • • • • • • • • •

It was really hot during the next team practice. Everyone was dripping with sweat as they worked their way through a series of drills and exercises.

"I think I'm melting in all this heat," Buster complained. "This is worse than being stuck in the desert."

Arthur wiped his forehead. "I'm sure I'm getting smaller," he said. "No one could lose this much water without shrinking."

Muffy sighed. "Don't remind me. I'd pay anything for a tall glass of ice cold lemonade."

"One glass?" said Francine. "I need ten."

After a few more minutes, the team got a break. Everyone sat down in the shade of a tree near the field.

"You guys will never get any better lying around like this."

Binky had arrived.

"Oh, look who's here," said Francine.

"Nice of you to join us," said the Brain.

"I didn't miss any of the scrimmage, did I?" asked Binky.

"No," said Francine. "But you should get here early enough to loosen up."

"But that's all so complicated," said Binky. "I just want to play ball."

"We all do," said Francine. "It just helps to prepare properly. Look at what we eat, for example. In the old days, athletes didn't connect good eating with good playing. They just ate whatever they felt like. On some days, Babe Ruth used to eat eight hot dogs before a game."

"Eight?" said Buster.

"My kind of guy," said Binky.

"Well, it was something like that," Francine went on. "And even though he played really well, he could have played even better. Now the top athletes have personal trainers and cooks."

"Which reminds me why I want to be a top athlete," said Muffy.

When the coach told them to start the scrimmage, the players broke into two teams and Francine's took the field.

Binky came to bat first, facing Francine on the mound.

"I'll bet you're as rusty as an old gate," she said.

Binky gripped his bat tightly. "Just pitch," he said.

Francine threw the ball — and Binky cracked a single to right field. As he stood on first base, he shook each of his legs.

Francine stared at him. "What are you doing?" she demanded.

"Just shaking off the rust," Binky explained.

As Francine's next pitch reached the catcher, Binky took off for second base. The catcher tried to throw him out, but the tag was too late.

"What did you think of that?" Binky asked.

The Brain was playing second base. "You showed good speed," he admitted, "but . . ."

"But what?" said Binky.

"Just remember, a sudden burst of speed puts a great strain on your muscles. They can get caught by surprise."

"I like surprising my muscles," said Binky. "It keeps them on their toes."

And just to prove his point, he stole third base after the very next pitch.

Chapter 4

• • • • • • • • • • •

"Here he comes," whispered Buster, who was keeping a sharp lookout.

Arthur nodded. They had invited Binky over to play, hoping to teach him a few things before it was too late.

As Binky rounded the corner, Buster ran up to him.

"It's terrible!" he shouted.

"What?" said Binky.

"A tragedy of colossal proportions!"

"WHAT?" Binky said again.

"The calamity of the century!"

Binky folded his arms. "What *are* you talking about, Buster?"

"Look!" cried Buster, pointing.

Arthur was sitting on the ground, shaking his head.

Binky rushed over. "Arthur, are you okay?" he asked.

Arthur sighed. "Oh, yes. I'm fine. But I can't say the same for the Amazing Stretch-O-Man."

He pointed down at the doll-sized figure in front of him. It seemed to be made of a jumble of rubber bands. Next to the figure were a few buildings. Looming over them all was a hanging Ping-Pong ball.

Binky frowned. "Who's that?" he asked.

"The latest superhero," Buster explained. "A friend of Bionic Bunny's. He has the ability to stretch himself into any shape — thick or thin, long or short."

"He doesn't look like much of a superhero," said Binky.

"Of course not," said Buster. "He's had a terrible accident."

"You see," said Arthur, "because the Amazing Stretch-O-Man is so flexible, it's almost impossible for him to get hurt. Almost everything just bounces off him. Even if some villain dropped a car on him, he would just squish down until the car was removed."

"So what happened here?" asked Binky.

"Well, Stretch-O — that's what we call him for short — was trying to rescue Fair City from the evil clutches of Dr. Destructo."

"Dr. Destructo?" said Binky.

"He's Stretch-O's greatest enemy," Buster explained. "Not very nice. A real meanie. The worst —"

"I *get* it," said Binky. "He's the bad guy."

"Exactly," said Buster. "Well, Dr. Destructo has diverted an asteroid to hit Fair City. Stretch-O was going to turn himself into a giant slingshot so that he could send the asteroid back into space."

"Sounds good to me," said Binky.

"It was a good plan," Arthur agreed. "Unfortunately, Dr. Destructo also has this invention, the Mind Bender, and he caught Stretch-O in it."

"Ooooh," said Binky. "Does the Mind Bender take control of his body and make him Dr. Destructo's slave?"

"No," said Arthur.

Binky looked disappointed.

"But it does make him forget to do things," said Buster. "Important things. And for Stretch-O, there's nothing more important than stretching. Normally, he takes a few minutes to stretch himself in every direction before he saves the world or whatever. That way he doesn't pull any muscles. But under the influence of the Mind Bender, he forgot."

"So now he's in trouble," said Arthur. "You see the point we're making?"

"Of course," said Binky.

"You do?" said Buster. "That's great."

Binky nodded. "Somebody else has to stop the asteroid from crashing into Fair City. I'll bet this is it."

He reached over, grabbed the Ping-Pong ball, and threw it into the bushes.

"There," said Binky. "Now I've saved the day for everyone."

"That's all?" asked Arthur.

Binky stopped to think. "Well, there is one more thing. . . ."

"What is it?" asked Arthur.

Binky smiled. "I could really use one of those Mind Benders myself," he said.

Then he walked away.

Chapter 5

• • • • • • • • • • • •

The next morning at school, Mr. Ratburn called for everyone's attention.

"Quiet down, class," he said. "It's time to get started. As you know, today we start presenting the spring science reports. To be fair, I've put all your names in a hat and picked out one pair to go first."

"I hope it's not us," Buster whispered to Arthur. "I'm not done yet."

"And that pair," Mr. Ratburn went on, "is Muffy and Francine."

Francine jumped up out of her chair. "We won!" she cried. "I can't believe it."

"Um, Francine . . . ," Muffy began.

"I never win anything. I enter all the contests. I make sure my name is spelled correctly. I'm very neat. But nothing seems to help. I —"

"Francine!" Muffy hissed.

"I'd like to thank everyone who made this possible. . . ."

"FRANCINE!"

"What?"

"We didn't exactly win anything," Muffy explained. "We just get to go first."

Francine thought about this. "Oh," she said, retaking her seat.

The two of them then went up to the front of the room. They put out their note cards and leaned some posters on the chalk rack.

"Our report is on muscles," Francine explained, pointing to a red blob she had drawn in the poster's upper right-hand corner. "Without them we would not be able to give this report."

"We all have a lot of muscles," Muffy added. "And they work for us twenty-four hours a day."

Buster raised his hand. "Even when we sleep?" he asked.

"Even then," Francine assured him. "After all, we use muscles to help us breathe. Almost all of our muscles are hidden under our skin. But one is not."

Francine stuck her tongue out at the class. Everyone laughed — even Mr. Ratburn.

"Muscles are very important parts of the body," said Muffy. "They take their orders from the brain, which sends them electrical commands. These commands trigger chemical changes that affect the muscle's actions. The brain is in charge of everything, like the *maître d'* at a fancy restaurant. The muscles are like the waiters — following orders and moving things around."

"Muscles work together," said Francine.

"There are more than six hundred muscle groups in the body. But like anything that works hard, muscles get tired. When a muscle moves a lot, it uses up oxygen and food. Your heart tries to keep the muscles satisfied, but it can't always keep up. That's when you need to rest."

Francine looked right at Binky. "Muscles also don't like doing things they're not used to. If you surprise your muscles with unexpected movements, your muscles may surprise you back."

"Muscles need to be pampered," Muffy explained. "Treat your muscles right, and they'll treat you right, too."

Binky just laughed. "You guys worry too much," he said. "Think strong. Be strong. I'm like Superman."

"Even Superman had to worry about Kryptonite," Arthur reminded him.

Binky laughed. "I'll take my chances," he said.

Chapter 6

· · · · · · · · · · · ·

The first game of the season, between the Eagles and the Penguins, drew a big crowd. The bleachers were filled with friends and families of both teams.

"Go, Penguins! Eagles can't get off the ground!"

"Eagles rule! Penguins get cold feet!"

The players themselves were sitting on the grass, stretching and flexing to loosen up.

"All ready for the big game?" Buster asked Francine.

She stared back at him. "Can't you tell by looking? This is my game face."

"It looks just like your regular face."

"Well, there's a difference," Francine insisted. "You have to look harder."

The Brain and Arthur were each kneeling on one leg with the other stretched out behind him.

"Are you nervous?" Arthur asked.

"A little," the Brain admitted. "Although I know it's an artificially created psychological condition, I can't help feeling that way when my parents are watching."

"Everybody's watching," said Binky, standing in front of them. "It's going to be a big game." He looked around. "I think I'll go see if anyone wants my autograph."

The game started in another few minutes. It moved quickly at first, with neither team scoring in the first two innings. In the third, Buster flied out, then Francine hit a single to left field.

This brought Binky to the plate.

"Come on, Binky!" Francine shouted. "Move me along."

Binky nodded and carefully set his feet in the batter's box.

The first two pitches were balls, but the third was a called strike.

"Two and one," said the umpire.

Binky dug in. As the next pitch came in, he swung hard.

Craaack!

The ball headed on a line toward center field. Francine took off, passing second base on her way to third.

Binky thought he might have a double if he hustled. He rounded first with an eye on the outfield. The center fielder was just picking up the ball.

"I can make it!" he muttered.

He churned his legs faster, trying to lengthen his stride.

Suddenly, Binky fell, going down in a cloud of dust.

"Come on, Binky!" Buster shouted. "You can still make it."

But Binky didn't move. At least he didn't get up. He was holding his leg and biting his lip.

A few moments later he was tagged out. The umpire called time, and Coach Frensky rushed to Binky's side.

"Who kicked me?" Binky asked.

"What do you mean?" asked the coach.

"I was running from first to second, and someone kicked me in the back of the leg."

The coach shook his head. "That's not what happened, Binky. There was no one near you."

"Well, it felt like somebody kicked me," Binky insisted.

The coach nodded. "When you pull a muscle, it can feel like that. Can you get up?"

Binky nodded. "I think so."

He leaned on Coach Frensky as he hobbled off the field.

The crowd cheered, glad to see Binky was okay.

But when the Eagles retook the field for the next inning, Binky was not with them.

Chapter 7

• • • • • • • • • • • •

"Look on the bright side," Buster said.

"There is no bright side," Binky growled.

They were standing outside Binky's house with Arthur and the Brain. It was the day after Binky had hurt his leg, and he was hobbling around. The others had come over to see how he was doing.

"What does it feel like?" the Brain asked.

Binky stopped to think. "Kind of stiff and hard. Like a knot I tied too tight."

"It could have been worse," said Arthur. "At least you didn't break anything."

"Yeah," said Buster, "it's not like you're

in the hospital waiting for a brain transplant."

"Uh, Buster," said the Brain, "there's no such thing as a brain transplant."

Buster nodded. "Which is why needing one would be so bad. Your chances would be bleak, hopeless. . . ."

"Well, this is bad enough," Binky insisted. "I can sort of walk, but going up or down stairs takes a while."

"Does it have a fancy name?" Arthur asked. "Your injury, I mean?"

Binky sighed. "No. It's just a pulled muscle."

"How long do you have to sit out?" the Brain asked.

"The doctor didn't say. 'People heal at different rates,' he said. 'You can't predict these things. Only time will tell.' "

The Brain looked at his watch. "Speaking of time, we have to get to practice. Um, are you coming?"

Binky looked down at his leg. "Maybe later. You go on ahead. I couldn't keep up, anyway."

"Okay," said Arthur. "We'll see you when you get there."

Binky watched his friends disappear around the corner.

Dr. Destructo let out an ugly laugh.

"So, Amazing Stretch-O-Man, how does it feel to be without your superpowers?"

"I've felt worse."

"Oh, really?" The doctor laughed again. "Actually, since you can't stretch anymore, perhaps I should just call you Binky Barnes."

Binky gasped. "You know my secret identity? How is that possible?"

"Evil has its ways, Mr. Barnes. Surely, you didn't expect that silly little mask to fool me for long. But my knowledge is the least of your problems. Look around you."

Binky's head did a slow turn. He was suspended off the floor in a steel cage. Below him

was a giant water tank filled with man-eating sharks. They were swimming in circles, their fins slicing through the water.

"Unusual pets, don't you think?" said Dr. Destructo. "Even if you could get out of the cage, you would still have to deal with the sharks. And I'm afraid I don't feed them very often.

"Of course, if you had your superpowers, escaping would be easy. But you don't, now do you?"

Binky frowned. "Well, I'll get them back."

Dr. Destructo took out his map of world domination. "I don't think so," he said, inspecting the position of his forces. "You've never faced this problem before. You might as well give up now."

He laughed again, and it was his ugliest laugh yet.

Chapter 8

● ● ● ● ● ● ● ● ● ● ●

For two days Binky stayed away from the baseball field. At school he didn't ask any questions about what was happening, and the other kids tried not to mention it.

But when Binky realized that his leg might take longer to heal, his curiosity got the better of him. So one afternoon he showed up, huddling behind the backstop as the team began its drills.

"Binky!" Coach Frensky ran over to say hello.

"How are you feeling?"

Binky stared at the ground. "Okay," he said.

"Glad to hear it." He lowered his voice. "Actually, you've arrived just in the nick of time."

Binky looked up. "I have?"

The coach nodded. "I don't know if you noticed, but this team is a long way from being where it should be. But I'm only one coach. I can only do so much." He sighed. "That's where you come in."

"Me?"

"I could really use an assistant, someone to help run the drills. Nothing permanent, you understand. Just until your leg feels better. What do you say?"

Binky stopped to consider it. "Do I get a whistle?"

"Probably not. I don't have one myself."

"Oh. Well, I guess I could do it, anyway."

"Excellent. I really appreciate it." Coach Frensky smiled. "Now let's go whip this team into shape."

Over the next few days Binky stepped in wherever the coach sent him. Now that he wasn't playing, he couldn't help noticing all of the time everyone spent getting ready before playing. It was really a lot of work. Still, he thought he could get them in better shape.

"Come on, Brain," he said. "You call that a wind sprint?"

"I'm making every effort," huffed the Brain.

Binky folded his arms. "You could have fooled me. A wind like that wouldn't even put out a candle. As for you, Arthur, get that glove dirty when you field a grounder. You need to lunge for the ball."

Arthur wiped the sweat from his forehead. "I'm lunging, I'm lunging."

"Yeah, yeah. . . . Bend those knees. You're not ready for a rocking chair yet. And, Buster, don't tell me your feet are nailed to the ground."

"Ugh!" said Buster. "I'm jumping as high as I can."

Binky just shook his head. "I wouldn't say that so loudly if I were you. When you leap for a line drive, you have to reach for the sky."

"Binky, over here!" called Coach Frensky.

"You guys keep it up," said Binky. "I'll be back later."

"Do you remember the old days?" Buster grunted as Binky walked away.

"The old days?" gasped Arthur.

"Before Binky cared about all this stuff?"

Arthur nodded. "It seems like only yesterday."

"Well," said Buster, "I'm glad Binky has changed his thinking, but you know what?"

"What?"

"Sometimes," said Buster, "I miss those days."

Arthur sighed. Sometimes, he missed them, too.

Chapter 9

• • • • • • • • • • •

But while yelling from the sidelines filled Binky's practices, he was not allowed to do the same thing during the games. He had to sit on the bench and mostly keep his comments to himself. It was torture to see a runner on third with two out and not be able to come to the plate. And it was painful to watch a line drive headed for the gap and have no chance to catch it.

So Binky decided he needed to help his recovery along. After everyone went home from the games, he stayed behind. He made up his own series of drills and steadily went through them. And each time he tried, he was able to do a little better.

It was not until after the second game that he was discovered.

"What are you doing?"

Binky had been sitting on the ground with one leg bent under him and the other stretched out before him. Now he looked up to see D.W. watching him closely.

"What are you doing here, D.W.?"

"I came back for my hat. I left it on the bench."

"So now you can go," said Binky. "Bye."

She just stood there. "You didn't answer my question. But that's okay. . . . I already know the answer. I *know* what you were doing."

"What?"

D.W. folded her arms. "You were stretching."

"No, I wasn't."

"I saw you."

46

"Well, maybe you need glasses."

"Come on, Binky. You'll have to do better than that. I'm Arthur's sister, remember?"

"Okay, okay, so maybe I am moving my muscles around a little. The doctor said I could get better faster if I worked at it."

"So, does it help?"

Binky frowned. "I think so. I'm not supposed to force anything."

"Well, I hope it works," said D.W. "The team needs you."

Binky beamed. "Thanks, D.W. Um, I was wondering. Do you think my exercising could be our little —"

"Secret?" D.W. finished for him. She nodded. "I love keeping secrets, especially from Arthur."

"Good," said Binky. And he went back to work.

Crash!

"What's this?" said Dr. Destructo, entering his evil lair.

His steel cage was sitting in the water tank with all the sharks trapped inside.

"Sorry," said Binky, "my superpowers have returned. I am once again the Amazing Stretch-O-Man."

"But how? Your injury was so great!"

Now it was the Amazing Stretch-O-Man's turn to laugh. "You made a serious mistake, doctor. You underestimated my ability to bounce back from even the worst situations."

"Curses!" shouted the doctor. "You may have won this round, Stretchbuster, but I'll be back to ruin another day."

Dr. Destructo pressed a secret button in the wall and dropped through a trapdoor that sealed shut behind him.

"We may meet again, Dr. Destructo," said the Amazing Stretch-O-Man, to himself. "But next time, I'll be ready."

Chapter 10

. . . .

Binky took a deep breath. He had returned
to the Eagles' lineup, surprising everyone
but D.W. with his appearance.

"Are you sure you're okay?" asked
Coach Frensky.

"I'm sure," said Binky, and he took his
place on the bench.

"It's great that you're back," said
Arthur.

Francine nodded. "We all thought you'd
be out much longer."

"He's a quick healer," D.W. explained
with a smile.

Binky was scheduled to bat fifth. When

he came up, there were two outs and Francine was on third base.

"Come on, Binky!" she shouted. "Bring me home!"

Binky took his stance at the plate. He felt a little nervous looking at the spot between first and second, the spot where he had fallen almost one week before. He gripped the bat firmly, and waited.

Three pitches later, he was out.

"You'll get it next time," said Arthur.

The next time Binky came up, he hit a grounder that the shortstop backhanded deep in the hole. Binky ran toward first, but he could feel himself still holding back.

He was out by a step.

"Good try!" said Buster.

Binky kept his head down and rubbed the dirt out of his eye.

The game was tied, 4 – 4, when he came up for the third time. He stared at the pitch all the way in — and rapped it into the gap in left center.

"Go, Binky, go!" the team shouted.

As he rounded first, Binky could see the left fielder just coming up with the ball. He could make it, he thought, he just had to pour on the speed. He ran right past the place where he had fallen and slid into second just under the throw.

"Safe!" declared the umpire.

Binky called for time, and then dusted himself off. He had made it! And more important, he hadn't hurt himself in the process.

"Nice slide!" shouted Francine.

"You really stretched that one!" the Brain called out.

Binky smiled. "I've been practicing," he said.

As Muffy came to the plate, Binky bent his front leg and rocked back and forth to

stay loose. The Brain gave him a big thumbs-up from the bench.

And when Muffy hit the next pitch up through the middle, he was off and running with the crack of the bat.